A BILLY AND BLAZE BOOK

Blaze and the Indian Cave

WEEKLY READER CHILDREN'S BOOK CLUB · · PRIMARY DIVISION

BLAZE and the Indian Cave

Story and Pictures by C. W. ANDERSON

THE MACMILLAN COMPANY, NEW YORK

COLLIER-MACMILLAN LIMITED, LONDON

To Crawford
and David Taisey

Billy was a boy who had a pony named Blaze that he loved very much. Blaze was very gentle and obedient, and Billy took the best care of him. They often took long rides and explored the country.

One day Billy's cowboy friend Jim told him about an Indian cave up in the hills.

"I often camped there when I was a boy," said Jim. "I liked to see the pictures the Indians painted on the walls long ago."

Billy's father and mother said he
could camp there overnight if he was
very careful about his fire. So, early
the next morning, he packed food
in a blanket and set out for the hills.

Blaze went along very eagerly.
He liked exploring too.

After riding many miles they came
to the hills, and there, far away, Billy
could see the cave.

"This is going to be very exciting,"
he said to Blaze. "I have never seen
an Indian cave."

Blaze hurried along, and soon
they were there.

As soon as they got to the cave,
Billy hurried inside with a flashlight.
There on the walls were pictures of
Indians and buffalo and deer.

How long ago they must have
been painted! But the colors
were still bright.

Then Billy tied Blaze to a small tree
in a place where he could graze. Later
he watered the pony at a spring nearby.
They had come a long way, and both were
hungry and thirsty.

Billy rested in the shade until
the sun went down and then built
a small fire and made his supper.
The food always tasted so good
when he cooked outdoors. He ate
a big meal and soon began to
feel sleepy.

Using his saddle as a pillow, the
way cowboys do, he lay thinking
of the Indians who once lived there.
It must have been very exciting
when big herds of buffalo were on
the prairie and deer could be seen
everywhere. The last thing he
thought of before he fell asleep
was Blaze grazing quietly outside.

He was very tired and slept soundly.

When he awoke, it was bright daylight.

He sat up, put on his hat—

and suddenly his heart seemed to stop.

There was no Blaze outside.

His lasso lay by the tree, but Blaze
was nowhere in sight. Billy knew
his pony would never leave him,
even if he got loose.

Someone had stolen him!

Billy could see tracks of the pony's feet, and he followed them. Even though he knew he could never catch up, he felt he must try to get Blaze back. He had to.

After going a long way, he saw a man on horseback. When Billy came up to him, he saw that he was an Indian with a very wrinkled face. Billy told him about Blaze.

"Maybe Joe Rattlesnake stole your pony," said the old Indian. "He's a no-good Indian."

They followed the tracks together,
and Billy was surprised at how much
the old Indian could tell from them.

"Here your pony tried to turn back.
He didn't want to go away from you."

When they came to a high ridge, they
could see a man on horseback far away.
Even at that distance, Billy knew
it was Blaze he was riding.

"We'll catch him," said the old Indian.

The Indian told Billy that Joe
Rattlesnake would have to come out
of the valley through a narrow canyon.
If Billy hurried, he could head him off.
The old Indian would chase him.

"Can you throw a lasso?" asked
the Indian.

Billy nodded.

Billy took the short cut the old Indian
pointed out and hurried as fast as
he could. If he could only get to that
canyon before Blaze and Joe Rattlesnake!

Billy dashed down into the canyon
and hid behind a big rock. Soon he
heard hoofbeats, and there was Blaze.
He did not want to go any farther,
so Joe Rattlesnake was whipping him
to make him go on.

When they came closer, Billy
leaped up and called, "Whoa, Blaze!"
Blaze stopped short, and Billy
threw his lasso.

It caught Joe Rattlesnake around the chest. Billy pulled as hard as he could, and Joe Rattlesnake came tumbling to the ground.

The fall stunned him. The old Indian came up and tied his hands behind his back.

"I'll take him to the sheriff," he said. "He won't be able to steal horses for a long time."

How happy Billy was as he rode toward home. He had his pony again. In his pocket he carried a beautiful red arrowhead that the old Indian had given him.

"Good-luck arrowhead for a good brave boy," he had said.

Billy was very proud and happy.